DISCARD

Dr. Clock-sicle

MARTHA WESTON

Holiday House / New York

To Martha, in loving memory,
from her family
and to Ashley Wolff, Julie Downing, and Mary Cash
for finishing this book

Reading Level: 1.9

Text and illustrations copyright © 2004 by Martha Weston
All Rights Reserved
Printed in the United States of America
www.holidayhouse.com
First Edition
1 3 5 7 9 10 8 6 4 2

Library of Congress Cataloging-in-Publication Data
Weston, Martha.
Dr. Clock-sicle / Martha Weston—1st ed.
p. cm.
Summary: Dr. Clock and his baby travel back in time
to visit prehistoric animals in the Ice Age.
ISBN 0-8234-1825-1 (hardcover)
[1. Time travel—Fiction. 2. Glacial epoch—Fiction.
3. Woolly mammoth—Fiction. 4. Mammoths—Fiction.
5. Prehistoric animals—Fiction.] I. Title: Doctor Clock-sicle. II. Title.
PZ7.W52645Dr 2004
[E]—dc22
2003059140

Dr. Clock is going
back to the Ice Age.
He is going in his very own
time machine!

His baby wants
to come too.

3

"I want to see a saber-toothed cat,"
says Dr. Clock.

"But I have to be back for lunch!"

Dr. Clock is a scientist.

He is in a hurry.

Dr. Clock sets the dials.
He is ready to go.

The baby wants to go
in the time machine too.

Dr. Clock pushes the PAST button.
FISSITT!

Dr. Clock and his baby
are zipped back in time.
They go to the Ice Age.

"Yikes!" says Dr. Clock.
"The time machine
   is sliding on ice!"

Bump!
The time machine stops.

Dr. Clock climbs out.

Brrrr! The air is very cold.

Dr. Clock is in a hurry.

He wants to find a saber-toothed cat.

His baby is in a hurry.

His baby wants to get
out of the snow.

"Will I see a saber-toothed cat
from this snowy hill?"
asks Dr. Clock.
"Will I see a saber-toothed cat's food?"
A scientist is full of questions.

Dr. Clock climbs to the top.

But he does not see a big cat.

He does not see big-cat food.

"Hmm," says Dr. Clock.

"This snowy hill is warm.

This grass is funny.

I wonder why?"

A scientist is full of questions.

"Yikes!" says Dr. Clock.

"The snowy hill is moving!"

"Is it an earthquake?

Is it an avalanche?"

A scientist is full of questions.

Dr. Clock has some answers.
"This grass is not grass,"
he says. "It is hair.
This snowy hill is not a hill.
It has legs and tusks."

"It is a woolly mammoth!"

The woolly mammoth walks fast.

Dr. Clock is very cold.

He hangs on.

The baby gets out of the way.

A scientist does not
see everything.

Dr. Clock sees claw marks
high on a tree.

"Maybe a big cat did that,"
he says.

"Hmm," says Dr. Clock.
"A saber-toothed cat was here.
Is a saber-toothed cat near?"
Dr. Clock jumps.
It is a long way down.
"Brrrr!" he says.
"I'm as cold as
a Popsicle."

Dr. Clock looks and looks.

But he does not see

a saber-toothed cat.

A scientist does not

see everything.

"Oh, dear!" says Dr. Clock.

"It is lunchtime.

I must go back to my lab."

Squish!

"Uh, oh," says Dr. Clock.

"What did I step in?"

It looks like poop.

Animal poop is called scat.

"Hmm," says Dr. Clock.

"Is this big-cat scat?"

"What did the big cat eat?"
A scientist is full
of questions.
Dr. Clock puts
the scat in a jar.
"I can study this
in my lab," he says.
"I can find out
what the big cat ate!"

Rrrowl!

Dr. Clock sees
a saber-toothed cat!
It is lunchtime,
but Dr. Clock is not hungry.
Now he has a new question.

Is it lunchtime
for the big cat?

Dr. Clock does not wait
for an answer.
He hurries to the time machine.
The big cat hurries too.

Dr. Clock jumps inside.

He slams the door.

He sets the dials.

"To the lab!" says Dr. Clock.
He pushes the FUTURE button.
The baby comes too.
A scientist does
not see everything.

FISSITT!

Dr. Clock zips forward in time.

His baby zips forward too.

"Hi, Baby!" says Dr. Clock.
"I'm back in time for lunch.
 I went to the Ice Age.
 Look!
 Here is big-cat scat!"

Dr. Clock and his baby
eat lunch.
The baby has lots of
stuff in a hat.
"Baby," says Dr. Clock.
"What is all that?"

"Do I see big-cat teeth?"
asks Dr. Clock.
"Do I see rocks and bones?
Did you go to the Ice Age too?"

Scientists are full of questions.